# THE FALL FAIRY GATHERING

Liza Gardner Walsh

*Illustrated by* Hazel Mitchell

Down East Books

Camden, Maine

# Down East Books

Published by Down East Books
An imprint of
The Rowman & Littlefield Publishing Group, Inc.
4501 Forbes Blvd., Ste 200
Lanham, MD 20706
www.rowman.com

Distributed by NATIONAL BOOK NETWORK

Copyright © 2020 by Liza Gardner Walsh
Illustrations © 2020 by Hazel Mitchell

*All rights reserved. No part of this book may be reproduced in any form or by any electronic or mechanical means, including information storage and retrieval systems, without written permission from the publisher, except by a reviewer who may quote passages in a review.*

*ISBN 978-1-60893-592-5 (hardcover)*
*978-1-60893-593-2 (ebook)*

*British Library Cataloguing in Publication Information Available*

**Library of Congress Cataloging-in-Publication Data Available**

Library of Congress Control Number: 2019951109

Printed in Selangor Darul Ehsan Malaysia (April 2020)

ALL year long,
for so many reasons,
the fairies have been busy
in every season.

WINTER was filled with endless planning
and making sure the fairy houses were still standing.

SPRING was spent planting seeds and flowers,

watching them grow each and every hour.

SUMMER was nonstop,

exploring and having fun,

with activities to savor

in that hot summer sun.

But now fall is here, with its bright and festive glow,
and the world is ready to put on a most colorful show.

THE days cool, and the light starts to fade,

as leaves twirl, leap, and promenade.

AND as nature sets the stage for fall,
the fairies gather to hold a magical ball.

It is time to collect

each ripened berry

as the harvest begins

for each and every fairy.


Acorn caps, apples,

pumpkins galore,

cranberry sauce, cider,

carrots, and more.

FAIRIES come from the woods, ocean, mountains, and streams,
bearing endless treasures and to share fairy dreams.

THEY make a patchwork quilt of different fairy tribes,
each square different in appearance, clothing, and vibe.

THE oak fairies polish their stores of acorn caps,

so the maple fairies can fill them with syrupy sap.

THE berry fairies bring an assortment of fruit

to complement the apple fairies' red and gold loot.

THE flower fairies are laden with lovely bouquets

that the seashell fairies place in a periwinkle vase.

ONCE the table is set and the food is on display,

the fairies gather 'round, for there is much to say.

THEY feel lucky to be together
in this diverse group,
thankful for clean air, good friends,
and delicious harvest soup.

They pledge to continue
protecting the earth from harm
and to encourage the young
to keep seeking its charms.

There is much to do in the greater world still,
But at the fall gathering, for now,
the fairies have more than their fill.

# THINGS YOU CAN DO FOR FAIRIES IN THE FALL

Leave out a thimbleful of soup

Keep things tidy and
sweep away the falling leaves

Support monarch butterfly organizations
that help the monarchs on their journey

Make lots of fairy houses

Set out acorn caps for the fairies to use in their feasts

Leave out wool roving and feathers for chilly nights

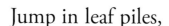

Jump in leaf piles,
but send a silent message to the fairies that you are coming

Don't break cobwebs

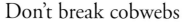